D0533846

and

Pet Rock

'I Am Strong!' and 'Pet Rock'
An original concept by Alison Donald
© Alison Donald

Illustrated by Camilla Frescura

Published by MAVERICK ARTS PUBLISHING LTD

Studio 11, City Business Centre, 6 Brighton Road,

Horsham, West Sussex, RH13 5BB

© Maverick Arts Publishing Limited November 2019

+44 (0)1403 256941

A CIP catalogue record for this book is available at the British Library.

ISBN 978-1-84886-626-3

www.maverickbooks.co.uk

This book is rated as: Red Band (Guided Reading)
This story is decodable at Letters and Sounds Phase 2.

I Am Strong!
and
Pet Rock

By **Alison Donald**

Illustrated by
Camilla Frescura

The Letter A

Trace the lower and upper case letter with a finger. Sound out the letter.

*Around,
up,
down*

*Down,
up,
down,
lift,
cross*

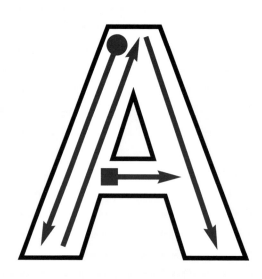

Some words to familiarise:

Lin   quick   doctor

High-frequency words:

is   I   is   a   has   up   as

Tips for Reading 'I Am Strong!'

- Practise the words listed above before reading the story.

- If the reader struggles with any of the other words, ask them to look for sounds they know in the word. Encourage them to sound out the words and help them read the words if necessary.

- After reading the story, ask the reader who Lin chooses to be in the end.

Fun Activity

Play dress up!

This is Lin. Lin can kick.

"I am strong!" Chop, chop!

Lin is a cat.

"I am quick!" Zip, zap!

Lin has a doctor's kit.

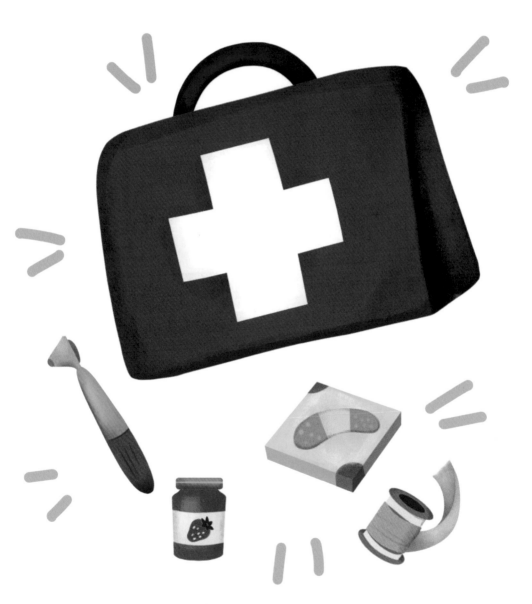

"I am clever!"

Lin has a wig.

"I am fun!" Bang, bang!

Lin is strong, quick,
clever and fun.

So Lin will dress up as...

...Lin.

"I am strong, quick, clever and fun."

The Letter P

Trace the lower and upper case letter with a finger. Sound out the letter.

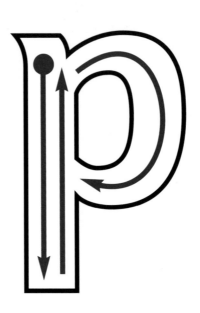

*Down,
up,
around*

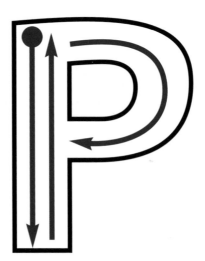

*Down,
up,
around*

Some words to familiarise:

rock   jacket   pocket

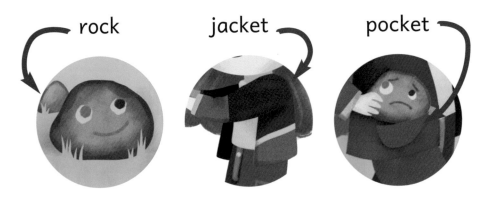

High-frequency words:

is   the   to   her   in

a   my   your   no

Tips for Reading 'Pet Rock'

- Practise the words listed above before reading the story.

- If the reader struggles with any of the other words, ask them to look for sounds they know in the word. Encourage them to sound out the words and help them read the words if necessary.

- After reading the story, ask the reader how Lin lost her pet rock.

Fun Activity

Make your own pet rock!

Pet Rock

This is Lin's pet rock.

Lin's pet rock likes the van.

Lin's pet rock likes to kick.

Lin's pet rock likes to run.

Lin puts her pet rock
in her jacket pocket.

Lin's pet rock does not
like the jacket pocket.

Lin gets a shock.

Where is my pet rock?

Book Bands for Guided Reading

The Institute of Education book banding system is a scale of colours that reflects the various levels of reading difficulty. The bands are assigned by taking into account the content, the language style, the layout and phonics. Word, phrase and sentence level work is also taken into consideration.

Maverick Early Readers are a bright, attractive range of books covering the pink to white bands. All of these books have been book banded for guided reading to the industry standard and edited by a leading educational consultant.

Pink
Red
Yellow
Blue
Green
Orange
Turquoise
Purple
Gold
White

To view the whole Maverick Readers scheme, visit our website at

www.maverickearlyreaders.com

Or scan the QR code above to view our scheme instantly!